MY FATHER'S
$\mathcal{H}$ANDS

WRITTEN BY SHEILA McGRAW & PAUL CLINE
ILLUSTRATED BY SHEILA McGRAW

A PETER SMITH BOOK FOR MEDLICOTT PRESS

Library of Congress Number
91-066764

ISBN 0-9625261-6-9

A Medlicott Press Book
Distributed by Green Tiger Press,
Simon and Schuster Building.
1230 Avenue of the Americas
New York, New York 10020

Edited by Kathleen Roulston, Toronto.
Designed by Sheila McGraw, Toronto.
Typeset by Satellite Compositors, Toronto.

Manufactured in Hong Kong

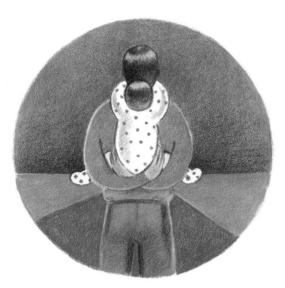

For Richard Frank Smith

— P.C.

For David Peter McGraw

— S.Mc.

My father's hands
are bigger than I am.

They gently and carefully
hold my future.

When I was new, my father learned
to feed me, burp me and change my diaper.
He would bathe me, rub me dry with my
fluffy towel and puff me with a cloud of powder.

He bought a camera
to take lots
of pictures and
he bought me piles
of toys, even though
I was much too little
to play with them.

My dad carried me like a football. He would tuck
me under his arm and hold my head in his hand.
He was always careful with me.

My father's hands
     build my confidence.

They hold me, guide me,
     catch me when I fall.

Soon I could run and climb on everything.
I rode on my father's back like a horse and on his
shoulders like a giraffe. Sometimes he held me up
high in the air. It made my tummy tickle.

My dad called
me Little Guy
and he taught me
to eat with a spoon.
Sometimes the
spoon was a train
and my mouth
was the tunnel.

Sometimes the spoon was an airplane and my mouth
was the hangar where the planes would park.
My dad always said *open wide Little Guy*.

My father's hands
are safe and secure.

They comfort and protect me.

When I started school, my father took me there every day. He showed me how to look both ways and safely cross the street. In the summer we went to the park to run around, paddle in the pool, throw my frisbee and play ball.

When we played catch, I would wear my big baseball glove. Whenever I missed the ball, my dad said *that was a close one.*

In the winter, we went to the park to skate. Afterwards, we would drink hot chocolate and hug each other to get warm. My dad's whiskers tickled and scratched at the same time. I called him Sandpaper Face.

My father's hands
      are gentle and kind.

They teach me
      how to care.

One day I went with my father to work.
All of his friends called me Bud. I was proud.

My dad and I liked to arm wrestle. I *nearly* won
every time. Sometimes
I would play with my
friends and sometimes
I would help my dad
around the house.
Usually I got
very dirty. My dad
always said

he was going to put me in a shopping cart
and send me through the car wash.
Then he'd chase me all around.
It was fun.

My father's hands
don't give up.

They show me how to build
my life, one piece at a time.

My father took me and my friend Jimmy camping. We piled our tent, sleeping bags and lots of other stuff into the car and drove far from the city, until we came to the campsite. It smelled so good there.

My dad showed us how to chop wood and how to build a fire. He put worms on our hooks and Jimmy caught a big fish. My dad cleaned it and cooked it for breakfast.

At night it was very, very quiet and very, very dark. There were so many stars and fireflies. We took turns telling ghost stories. There was no TV, but I didn't miss it. Some day I want to go back there.

My father's hands
are patient.

They hold understanding
and forgiveness.

When I started high school, I got a new haircut and new clothes. I started listening to different music. My voice got lower, except for the times when it went very high. Whiskers started to grow on my face and suddenly I grew very tall. My dad liked to tease me about all this new stuff. I teased him too, by calling him Dadosaurus Rex because he was so old fashioned.

I learned to drive and I started to like girls, especially Jennifer. People came to my school to talk to us about the future. There were people from colleges, the army and big companies. There were so many exciting things to do and so many scary choices to make.

My father's hands are strong.

They hold respect,
humility and dignity.

Then, when I was grown,

   I had to leave my father's hands
      in order to find them again.

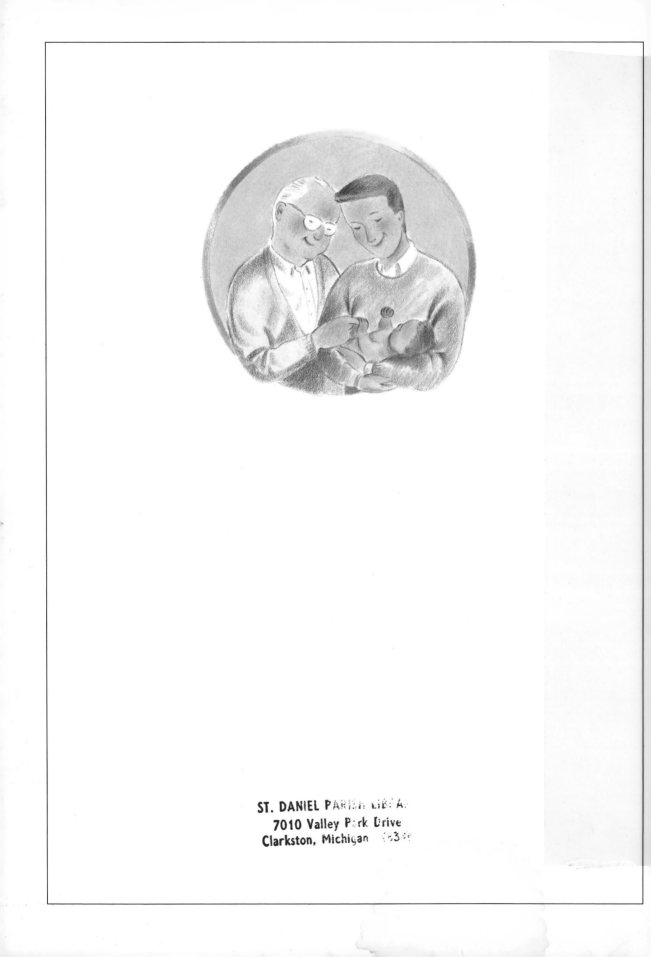